Roz Rock Star

by Liza Charlesworth

ISBN: 978-1-338-89038-9

Designer: Cynthia Ng; Illustrated by John Lund

1 2 3 4 5 6 7 8 9 10   68   31 30 29 28 27 26 25 24 23 22

Printed in Jiaxing, China. First printing, January 2023.

Ready to read a cool story?
Say hello to Roz.
Roz likes music A LOT
and has big dreams.
She wants to be a rock star!

So, Roz gets to work.
First, Roz learns to sing.

Then, Roz learns to play the guitar.
Strum, strum, strum!

Then, Roz learns to play the drums.
Bang, bang, bang!

Then, Roz learns to play the keyboard.
Plink, plink, plink!

"Cool!" says Roz. "I know how to sing.
I know how to play the guitar, the drums,
and the keyboard, too.
I'm all set to be a rock star."
So, Roz decides to have a concert.

Roz rolls out on the stage
and she begins to sing a song.

Then, Roz picks up the guitar
and begins to strum.

Then, Roz rolls over
and bangs on the drums.

Then, Roz rolls over
and plinks on the keyboard.

Guess what?
Roz can only play one instrument at a time,
so her band doesn't sound good AT ALL.
This makes Roz upset and she cries,
"My plan to be a rock star isn't working!"

Luckily, Roz's pal Matt hears her cry
and rolls over to help out.
"I can play the guitar," he says.
Strum, strum, strum!
"You sound awesome!" says Roz.

9

Then, Roz's pal June rolls
over to help her out.
"I can play the drums," she says.
Bang, bang, bang!
"You sound awesome!" says Roz.

Then, Roz's pal Dave rolls
over to help her out.
"I can play the keyboard," he says.
Plink, plink, plink!
"You sound awesome!" says Roz.

Roz had planned to be a rock star all by herself,
but her pals did sound pretty awesome.
So Roz says, "OK, you guys can join my band."
Roz and her pals get to work.
They practice. They jam.
They write lots of hip songs.

And Roz learns an important lesson.
"Music is SO much better when
you make it with your friends.
This is not MY rock band,
it is OUR rock band!" she says.

Then, Roz and Matt and June and Dave
decide the time is right to have a concert.
So, they roll out onto the stage
and do an AMAZING show!

Matt plays the guitar. *Strum, strum!*
June plays the drums. *Bang, bang!*
Dave plays the keyboard. *Plink, plink!*
And Roz sings loud and proud and strong.

Guess what?
Their concert is a HUMONGOUS hit!
Roz and Matt and June and Dave
all become famous rock stars.
Now, that is really cool.